For V, my favorite collaborator, and for Ma, my original editor
—B. L. H.

For Ladygirl, who somehow puts up with all of my shenanigans
—S. H.

ATHENEUM BOOKS FOR YOUNG READERS

An imprint of Simon & Schuster Children's Publishing Division

1230 Avenue of the Americas, New York, New York 10020

For information about special discounts for bulk purchases, please contact

Simon & Schuster Special Sales at 1-866-506-1949 or business@simonandschuster.com.

The Simon & Schuster Speakers Bureau can bring authors to your live event.

For more information or to book an event, contact the Simon & Schuster Speakers Bureau

at 1-866-248-3049 or visit our website at www.simonspeakers.com.

Book design by Ann Bobco

The text for this book was set in Quimbly Bold.

The illustrations for this book were illustrated with a combination of

pencil, ink, watercolor, and gouache.

Manufactured in China

0518 SCP

First Edition

2 4 6 8 10 9 7 5 3 1

Library of Congress Cataloging-in-Publication Data

Names: Hellman, Blake Liliane, author. | Henry, Steven, 1962- illustrator.

Title: Something smells! / Blake Liliane Hellman ; illustrated by Steven Henry.

Description: First edition. | New York : Atheneum, [2018] | "A Caitlyn Dlouhy book." |

Summary: When Elliot wakes up to a terrible smell, he is determined to find the source.

Identifiers: LCCN 2016045331| ISBN 9781481488648 (hardcover : alk paper) |

ISBN 9781481488655 (eBook)

Subjects: | CYAC: Odors—Fiction. | Cleanliness—Fiction. | Clothing and dress—Fiction. |

Family life—Fiction.

Classification: LCC PZ7.1.H4468 Som 2018 | DDC [E]—dc23

LC record available at https://lccn.loc.gov/2016045331

Something Smells!

by Blake Liliane Hellman

illustrated by Steven Henry

A CAITLYN DLOUHY BOOK

Atheneum Books for Young Readers

New York London Toronto Sydney New Delhi

WITHDRAWN

Early one morning,
Elliot woke up
to a most terrible smell.

He looked around his room
and frowned.

Something smells, he thought.

He checked under his bed.

But it was *perfectly* clean.

Was it a skunk?
He opened the window.

But the neighborhood smelled like fresh morning air.

He sniffed Mr. Jiggles.
But Mr. Jiggles didn't smell.

Pee Wee didn't smell.

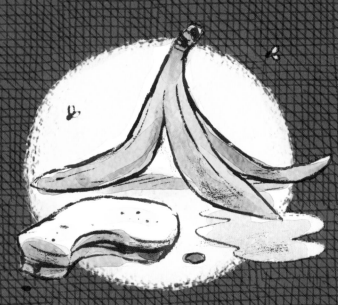

Wednesday's snack
didn't smell—
not very much, anyway.

Elliot could not find
the smell that smelled.

Maybe it's Dad,
he thought.

But Dad smelled pretty nice.

At breakfast his mother scolded him.

"Not one more day in that costume, Elliot!"

But he didn't want to take it off.
It was the best costume ever.

It glowed in the dark and happened to be
an EXACT REPLICA OF HIS SKELETON.

Besides, he was much
too busy hunting for
the terrible smell.

Dogs smell, he thought.
But Digsy smelled like bacon.

Little sisters smell.
But Lucy smelled like maple syrup.

He bet a million jillion jelly beans
it was the baby.

But Lilac smelled like baby powder.

Was it the cat food?

Nope.

Maybe it was the trash.

But all he found was some old Halloween candy.

What, what, **what**
was that terrible smell?!

Grandma's famous

Gefartzenschnaffel

Do you know what's

IN

Gefartzenschnaffel?

Neither did Elliot.

But that *wasn't* the smell
that smelled.

He looked up
in the attic . . .

and down in the basement . . .

and every place in between.

"Not one more second in that costume, young man!" said his mother.

"It's time for your bath!"

Elliot was disappointed he had not solved
the mystery of the terrible smell.

"Something smells," said Lucy.

"Something smells," said Grandma.

Elliot lathered and scrubbed and sudsed,
and when he was done . . .

SOMETHING swirled right down the drain.

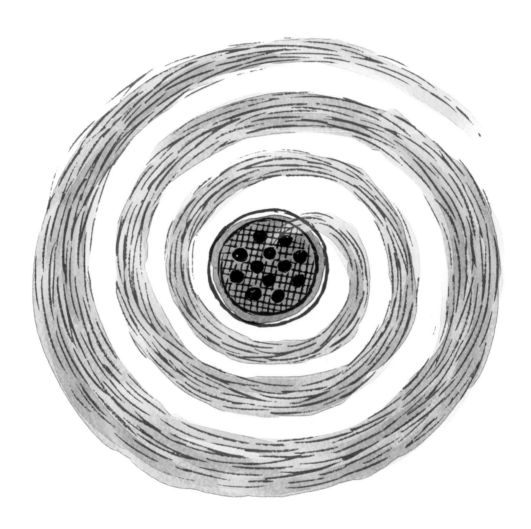

The terrible smell was gone.

After his bath,
Elliot was excited to put on
his new sea monster pajamas.

They were the best pajamas ever!
They had ACTUAL SCALES
and BIG, SCARY CLAWS!

They felt so good . . .

. . . he was never ever going to take them off.